Reycraft Books
55 Fifth Avenue
New York, NY 10003

Reycraftbooks.com

Reycraft Books is a trade imprint and trademark of Newmark Learning, LLC.

This edition is published by arrangement with China Children's Press & Publication Group, China.
© China Children's Press & Publication Group

Educators and librarians: Our books may be purchased in bulk for promotional, educational, or business use. Please contact sales@reycraftbooks.com.

This is a work of fiction. Names, characters, places, dialogue, and incidents described either are the product of the author's imagination or are used fictitiously. Any resemblance to actual persons, living or dead, is entirely coincidental.

Sale of this book without a front cover or jacket may be unauthorized. If this book is coverless, it may have been reported to the publisher as "unsold or destroyed" and may have deprived the author and publisher of payment.

Library of Congress Cataloging-in-Publication Data is available.

ISBN: 978-1-4788-6803-3

Printed in Dongguan, China. 8557/0721/18095

10 9 8 7 6 5 4 3 2

First Edition Hardcover published by Reycraft Books 2019

Reycraft Books and Newmark Learning, LLC, support diversity and the First Amendment, and celebrate the right to read.

REYCRAFT
BOOKS

Dragon's Hometown

ILLUSTRATED BY HECHEN YU

BY DONG HONGYOU

I was born in a magical land filled with beautiful dragons. At least, that's what I always imagined from the stories my dad told me. My birthplace sounded so wonderfully mysterious.

I always dreamed of going back for a visit. I wanted to see the dragons. In fact, I talked about it so much, my mom and dad gave me the nickname *"Little Dragon Girl."*

One day, my dream came true!

My parents and I made the long journey back to our old hometown. We flew from Los Angeles to China, and then set sail for Dragon Gate Island.

Far in the distance, my dad pointed out two huge rocks rising
out of the water, facing each other. Dad explained that on
Dragon Gate Island, the rocks were known as the Dragon Arch.

I couldn't wait to get to the island! We were arriving just
in time for the Lantern Festival, my favorite part of the
New Year celebration.

When we landed on the island, it was abuzz with excitement. Every house was beautifully decorated for the New Year. Grandma met us at the door and hugged me.

"Ah, my Little Dragon Girl's back!"

Grandpa was in the yard, painting the dragon for the dragon dance. Every year during the Lantern Festival, Grandpa is the one who gets to control the head during the dance. I grabbed Grandpa's hand and begged him to stop painting and take me to look for dragons. He hugged me and whispered,

"On the night of the Lantern Festival, we'll slip away and I'll take you dragon hunting!"

In the kitchen, Grandma wrapped dough made from rice flour around sweet fillings to form tangyuan. I had never seen so many of these treats in one place before!

Later, my cousin took me out to explore the island on stilts.

"Have you ever seen a dragon?" I asked him. "That's a secret!" he laughed as we teetered along.

Then we put on masks and marched up and down the street. Fish and meat were hanging on strings, drying in the sun.

The whole street smelled salty and yummy, and I started getting hungry. It was time to go home for lunch.

Early the next morning, the thunderous sounds
of fireworks and drums rang through the air.

The Lantern Festival had begun!

Grandpa checked one last time to make
sure the dragon was painted perfectly.
My dad took over Grandpa's place at the
dragon's head and led it in a graceful,
swooping dance through the air.

I dressed up as the legendary lotus-picking girl and carried a float
in the shape of her boat to the square. All eyes were on me.

I felt like a star!

When night fell, the island and lake
glowed with the light of many lanterns.

My family gathered around the table and feasted on an assortment of tangyuan. There were ones stuffed with red beans, black sesame, lotus seeds, and carrots. They were so sweet and delicious!

After we devoured the last of the tangyuan, Grandpa gave me a wink. It was time to release the lanterns . . . and look for dragons! I couldn't wait to spot one.

My cousin and I climbed into a little boat filled with
flickering lanterns. We sat down as Grandpa

paddled toward Dragon Arch. I wished we could paddle

faster, but Grandpa seemed to enjoy taking his time.

Finally, Grandpa stopped right in front of Dragon Arch. He got ready to place several lotus lanterns on the water.

I was surprised to see tiny tangyuan piled in the center of the petals. They looked just like pearls. "Grandpa!" I cried. *"Are these tangyuan for the fish?"*

"Oh yes," Grandpa replied.

"The fish celebrate the Lantern Festival, too. When they eat tangyuan, they get the strength they need to jump over the arch. That's how they turn into dragons!"

Soon the lanterns were floating around our boat. Suddenly, the surface of the water seemed to bubble up, and fish began leaping out. A huge orange carp jumped right into my arms!

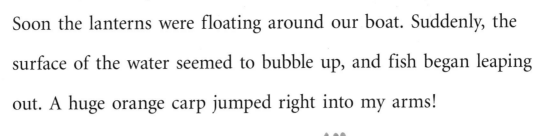

"Quick, put him back!" said Grandpa. "He's trying to jump over Dragon Arch!"

The yellow moonlight glistened on the lake and the shadow of Dragon Arch shimmered. I watched as fish leaped high into the air, trying their best to become beautiful dragons.

That night, I dreamed I was a carp. I jumped

up and soared over Dragon Arch to become a

shining golden dragon!

Now I truly was a Little Dragon Girl.